Sir Alfred John,
Short Stories and Memoirs,
Excerpts from Sir Alfred John,
The Home Chef's Creative Cookbook,
Including Short Stories and Memoirs
First Edition

by Michael F. Munnings

Copyright © 2011

ISBN-13: 978-1463654634
ISBN-10: 1463654634

Printed in the United States of America

10 9 8 7 6 5 4

August 2011

www.SirAlfredJohn.com

For those who want to learn culinary,
those who want to be a Home Chef,
those professionals who so
diligently train others,
I dedicate this book.

Let your adventure begin.

Dedicated to
Joyce Camille Maffeo Munnings.
My wife.
My best friend.
My inspiration.
My Me-Lo.
My Life.

TABLE OF CONTENTS

Sir Alfred John
Short Stories and Memoirs

Signature Page

The Authors Personal Message

 My culinary training was somewhat painful. Mom and Dad were committed to an increasingly long work schedule to manage a mid-class living. At a very young age, I typically was a homebody, shy, seemingly without many friends. Sprouting quickly to nearly six feet I would wait for at least one of my parent's arrival in hope of tasting a hot dinner, which was becoming seldom as their work hours extended. Growing so rapid my stomach consistently sent my eyes wandering into the cupboards for its next fill. My thoughts were not thinking of nutritional value but tastes beyond the pan of boiling water. It became clear that my culinary interests began.

With money allowances for food limited to only the school lunch program, my hands-on culinary training started immediately as I entered the home. The refrigerator and cupboards would open simultaneously in an exciting way to find the next experimental mix. Any foods or condiments not moving or subject to the wear and tear of green moss would become a viable food source. Deciding on the desired flavor for that nights pre-dinner, a mix of left overs, fresh foods, spices, flours, vegetables, would be combined into one bowl. These creative mixtures mostly had good results but any young teens tongue would enjoy clashing one-bowl meals.

Father arrived home early in the evening hours and Mother much later so by default father was the home chef. Father had a farm raised culinary training. He proved to me if you could churn butter from scratch, grow fresh farm vegetables, raise small animal stock, with limited resources, you learn how to create flavorful dishes. In his tyme, he also learned to cook by experimentation.

Father would sometimes speak of past cooking methods and food selections given him by ancestry and friends. But in the 1930's during the recession it became most challenging, as for most people, to take the cheapest of foods and turn them into a upbeat tasty dinner. Survival changes the way you cook and this is what he talked of most. Since money and food were scarce people cooked what they could afford or what they bargained in trade, and he spoke proudly of how many shared leftover breads or extra food rations they would have. This grass root foundation planted immediately in my soul at a young age and started my desire to tenderize an undesired cut of meat or to bring out the best of flavor in food.

Later in life my interest weaned to researching my ancestry, its heritage and the foundation of my creative thinking. It became clear in the genealogy that current family names of John, Alfred, Fred, Ray, and others were similar to those surnames found in Norfolk, England. The trail led me to believe that the heritage traces back to a higher respected class of great England's society, which is a very artistic family.

But, I am not totally sure. What I do know for sure is arriving from England to America was my great grandfather whom I have a early gunpowder lamp photograph, a Blacksmith, and his son my grandfather, who became a corner store market owner and butcher. To his business desire for success the recession of the 1930's excused our family of early riches leaving only a short memory of the American dream and the pride of giving most of his grocery contents to the people of the recession. In England however, with great respect and regards, most of the English family flourished.

This book represents my family heritage, both past and present, and is an autobiography of my families life and mine. Although fictional characters are used, most stories are part of someones experience of life and those lost of life. The book is written around the creation and passion of the art of food culinary, spices, cooking, and the desire to help others with similar passion. It is expressed through the character Sir Alfred John sharing his values of family, farmland, animals, and his early vision of a bringing Great England into the forefront of trade. As time went on, he aged and matured becoming concerned with the social values and a growing political environment that placed he saw placing burden on humanity, trade, and whales.

This writing has made me aware that our lives and what happens to us are not that much different than others. The difference is we just live in a different environment and stature of living. I believe that all our descendants shared the same value and character as this book portrays, only in a different time or place, with different hearts, and beliefs. That believe comes as it is known that history always repeats itself.

The Author

Remember, the flavour of life
is held by the hand
which measures it,
so be creative with the spice!

Sir Alfred John

Narrative

Sir Alfred John
The Story

Sir Alfred John became widely known in the region as a culinary creator. He owned a 5000-acre horse-trading farm and trading depot in Norwich, Norfolk, located in the East Anglia region of Eastern England; where equestrian and cattle drives are common. Lakes, flowing into running streams to the river, and rich soil are plentiful. The land brings forth freshness in farm raised beef, pork, poultry, clear water fish, and hearty vegetables. The nearby Great Sea brought traditional trade and fish Captains into port to settle inside Lowestoft Harbor after catching abundant seafood from the saltwater.

His land was a temporary stop for cattlemen and horse traders who travelled over our great England's rough terrain. These Countrymen who passed through kept to rest on his land for sleep and nourishment, knowingly to mingle with other traders, and to enjoy his fine English Cook before traveling onward.

In past Olde England days of early 19th century the obtainment of gold and spices were collected by persons our England's wealth. The authoritarian Kings and Queens would order its ships a travel destined around the globe in obtainment of our worlds gold so to support their luxury of materialistic extravagances, but also knowing the same ships would return with belly full cargos of exotic plant spices to delight and entertain their palates and exotic tastes. The spices first delivered directly to our governance and rulers were a distributed treasure to those finest of men and the wealthiest of our great England.

Sir Alfred John, whose father started low in social class, found wealth by creatively using his Fathers land for cultivating its finest of resources. With this new wealth, he could now afford to craft his gifted artistry of culinary to create the most flavored feasts so to please his lucrative traveling stay and trade patrons. To do  so, he would always have a plentiful assortment and quantity of farmland animals, dairy, vegetables, and wines to make wholesome hearty meals. Over tyme, as crowds grew towards his banquets, he increased the farms cultivation with the world's most freshest and selective plant spices and herbs. And, for those plants that his soil and sun could not support, his new social status allowed him to now trade with the great England governing rulers.

Patrons who never experienced such fine worldly tastes of culinary in their own settled regions would travel extra distances to delight in his hearty and tendered meals. If the traveler did not have his own wealth to pay for its food and bed, Sir Alfred John would simply bargain a trade for readily available hunter fox furs.

As these patrons traveled onward with his spices and herbs beyond his land, Sir Alfred John Marinades, Rubs & Seasoning became a most popular staple throughout England. Countrymen throughout the land who shared the spice at their neighbors feasts soon wanted access to this fine fresh flavour and tenderizer. He met this increasing interest by packaging and distributing his goods using hired hands and horse buggy who delivered it to the destined towns.

In his delivery of spice, his original packaging was a small burlap sprinkling bag placed into larger burlap wrapping bag so to protect it from the sun and elements of  nature. Small heavy rocks were placed inside the burlap bag so to shake finely ground spices over the food. People loved the spice and its easiness of use. It truly made daily flavoring and tenderizing of food easy, simple, and most flavorful.

Today, the Sir Alfred John's tradition of freshness, all natural ingredients, and no chemical preservatives continues.

Mike and Joyce Munnings
Author (aka MasterChef Mike)
and Spouse (aka Sous MeLo)

Sir Alfred John

Courage

Michael's Manhood

A Story of Michael..........In Youth

My name is Michael. As a small boy growing up near Sir Alfred John's ranch, I was able to visit the land periodically with my fathers' permission. One day my family and I were invited to the ranch for dinner to celebrate my birthday at my new young age of 10 years.

I have two brothers, a father, and mother. We did not have any sisters but elder cousin Romaine, daughter of Sir Alfred John, was my best friend and heart-warmed sister, so I guess I didn't need one at my house.

On this day, I was excited to learn that my farming adulthood was to be crossed. Sir Alfred John asked me through the permission of my father if I would prepare the chickens and assist the dinner. What an honor to be considered from such a prestige ranch holder. It seemed like so many hours to wait to honor the request. I couldn't wait.

Early morning in the next day, I went to our fields to practice the holding and cuts of the butcher. I practiced for hours and hours. On trees, on twigs, on anything that looked like the neck of a chicken. In the late afternoon, I was ready.

With fathers help, I placed his newly purchased and very sharp knife in the cloth and secured it into the carriage into its safest position. My father helped the rest of the senior family into our carriage, and drove us to the ranch. We finally arrived in a about 40-minute speed. I was so excited when I saw the house approaching and its nearest hen house. Everyone was standing on the front porch waiting for our arrival so to cordially greet us. It was a fabulous and proud moment. I counted 12 total persons that would attend my fine feast.

Everyone went inside the house except me. I was too eager to see the hen house so I ventured into it and counted twelve hens. In my excitement and eagerness to become a man, I ran and grabbed the butcher tools from the carriage. Then I returned to the caged poultry finding it strange that the hens were quiet, seemingly tired of serving eggs that day. But, since this was my first tyme for preparation, less noise would be beneficial.

I entered the cage and looked at them with hunted eyes and they looked back at me in a non-caring way.

I took one hen at a tyme out of the pen and placed them behind the wooden barn which sat atop the hill.

I proceeded with the preparation. With one chop of my axe, I severed their neck so they would have no pain. Once headless their feet would kick, keeping a balance, and ran down the hill crest behind me. I figured to pick them up after I cleared the hen house, preparing twelve hens, one each for the twelve persons attending my birthday party.

When I finished, I cleaned the axe and placed it back into the carriage. I then proudly ran into the house eagerly awaiting recognition for what is so far my best achievement. As I entered the banquet room I shouted "Everyone, Everyone, come see what I have done! The hens are near prepared and will be ready soon after I pluck their feathers". A look of confusion and shock came across everyone in the room as they realized I did something without supervision.

Father in a confused way, "Son Michael, what did you do?"

To excited, I stumbled my words so to tell father of my achievement but I could not as my heart was racing. So I said "Come see father, I will show you. Everyone, come see!"

I grabbed Fathers hand proudly leading him and those who followed over to the hen house. Once I arrived, I told everyone my story, "I removed each hen out of the hen house, placed them over there and got them severed, ready for plucking, just like you do father. Just like you! Look, they ran down the hillside, I need to go get them."

Taking everyone to the hills edge I pointed downward to its open field but I did not see any hen. I became both confused and scared. I said "Father, I placed them here, each one of them. They were here and then they ran headless down the hill. They should be down there. Where are they Father? Where did they go?"

Father, with a reddish face of embarrassment or anger, said , "Son, hens can run headless for miles in any direction until they fall from exhaustion? They can be anywhere."

Sir Alfred John showing disbelief of what he is seeing, looked into my fathers eyes and said "Did Michael sever 12 hens in one butchering? Do you know these hens are my egg production, not the chickens for todays dinner?" Then, pointing downhill to a smaller wooden shed, said "That cage you see is holding only four. Enough to feed all of us."

Then, Sir Alfred John remembered Michael's young age starting thinking of his mistakes of youth and began an internally belly laugh. In a tone not to let me off the hook, Sir Alfred John challenged my manhood. He said, "My young Michael, just imagine how scared those chickens got seeing headless hens running by them? I am sure they are ready for battle to anyone who dare enter their cage. Maybe you should go into their cage to see their reaction. Can you do this for your father and I?"

Father, realizing Sir Alfred John's antics, started to play along. He encouraged me to do the same saying "Michael, go see what that cage has in store for you. It would be very entertaining to see if you survive the battle."

Soon, everyone else started telling me to go into the cage to face the unknown.

I was now in total fear of what four chickens might do if I dare go into their cage. Seeing visions of bird attacks entered my imagination.

So, I bettered myself as a man, and told all of them that "I prefer to retrieve the dinner I already prepared. I do not want to waste good food that I can get just by finding them"

With that quick thinking and narrow escape, I boldly proceeded with determination down the hill to the tree line. For over an hour I searched until I was able to bring back five out of the twelve hens. Ever since that moment of tyme, everyone treated me differently, not like a child.

On that day, I entered manhood. And, for the rest of my days, someone will continue to remind me about that day.

Sir Alfred John

Morals

Decisions

If...........

If I have strength of integrity........
             it will be my foundation.

If I have strength of confidence......
             it will be my courage.

If I have strength in knowledge......
             it will be my mastery.

If I have strength of self-direction...
             it will be my destiny.

If I have strength of spouse............
             it will be my significance.

If I have strength of family............
             it will be my reason.

If I have strength of teaching........
             it will be my gift.

If I remove the if............................
             I will be my person.

Sir Alfred John

Sir Alfred John

Animal Magnetism

Baconly and the Blanket

Memoirs of Sir Alfred John.......... The Perfect Bacon

As a rancher, you become close to animals and they sometimes can become close to you. I must remember these loving creatures are Gods gentle creatures of our earth but reside on my land and do not know their purpose. Their tyme of stay is temporary so to support my family need for life's nourishment. As an old tyme rancher, I learned early in life not to directly look deeply into their eyes so not to forget their duty, but sometimes I h a r m l e s s l y a n d helplessly do so. Not to say that one animal becomes unique in their attempt to fill my heart with lovingness, b u t I a d m i t, I sometimes slip in my focus. I admit having  earthly feelings to different personalities, either animal or mankind. As I once was young, I see my children in their early years learning the same, and see that I will always connect passion in this childless way. I still seem to communicate verbally in voice and movement of body that makes you understand animal language. No matter how the connection comes, it always becomes playful, eye to eye, somehow understanding each other.

For example, my horse Trotter travels me to my farm and travel destinations, My dog Michol, protects our land from uninvited guests and natures unwanted attack animals. My herds of sheep keeps the field grass low so it can be walked on. But, my elder pig Baconly has confused me most with human mannerism.

Baconly is one who crafts an outsized smiling expression when we go to the pen to visit or feed. It seems Baconly will communicate with his face, squealing voice, and his head always shaking back and forth or up and down as he agrees or disagrees with your talking. His accuracy in his movement is highly accurate and remarkable as though he has learned and understands our great language.

Baconly is a wanderer. One who likes to escape continually from his pen by digging, knocking down a gate, or simply opening it in a number of curious ways. The lands ranch hands have made many repairs of the pen over the years but Baconly always finds his way. His continuing challenge is fun for us but at tyme annoying, and I keep him because his freedom and exploratory spirit is amusing. His unbelievable liveliness keeps me from making this sidekick a delicious dinner. Nevertheless, as a rancher I know someday that I must determine his fate.

One day in Baconly's later years, he finally made one of his fun filled adventures a nuisance to our farming budget. Aged fully and now cranky, he decided to destroy the complete pen from one end to the other. Not a post would be secure with Baconly's unique size and strength. Every side of the pen destroyed or knocked down but not for him to escape, only destroy, suggesting he is strongly angered. Having spent many hard-earned pounds to support him and his continual destruction of the pen, he is now over burdening the farm financially. So, I annoyed by his aggressiveness, made my decision. He will be in slaughter.

I thought it to be fair that I would respect him with my telling my dear old friend of his coming fate. When I told him, he shook his head up and down as to agree to conclude his fate. I told him the following day would be his tyme. He smiled again. I told him "Baconly, you are unique; you always seemed to understand me. I appreciate that. Thank you my dear friend."

So during this same night, Michol, my dog barked so many tymes but I noticed it in such a friendly way. It was a harmless passionate bark, so I thought little of it and fell asleep with my wife Joyce aside me.

As morning broke, I woke to a stale smelly heated air that yielded my bed and body to sweatiness. It felt like having heavy sheets and pillows to solidify my movement. Upon my eyes wakening to the sunrise light, I immediately looked down to see the strangest event ever, Baconly was laying down comfortably at the foot of my bed with his head up and looking directly at me. He had his usual wide-open eyes and his distinctive beaming smile that he displayed from ear to ear.

I immediately shouted at him with a screeching surprise, "Baconly! What are you doing in my bed?" Upon seeing him though, I finally realized how this smart animal outsmarted me during our lifetime together. Is he smarter than all pigs and possibly smarter than I am? He always expressed his emotions but just not the same as I do. Looking back, I concede he always gave the ranch his life, such as his zest for pig life, commotion, and his never-ending attempt to attract our attention. In addition, my realization Baconly hears my voice or sees my movements in such a way as to communicate. I finally realize that his lifetime pen destroying effort was his way to get close to us and show us he has a loving heart, even though we are so different. He must have hurt so much with our avoidance. But now at this moment he looks his happiest.

As I stayed staring at him and him staring back at me for what to be a forever still moment placed in tyme.

I said, "Baconly, I realize what you wanted from us." Just to be free and part of our family. I can now hear your voice saying something pig-lish. I now understand you have love for us. I am such a fool avoiding you all my life. I am sorry. I would like you to stay on the land freely. Freely without a cage surrounding you? I will change my decision and allow you your natural life to be long to age.

Thank you for allowing me to see this in you and awakening me to your desire for love as well. You are large and pink, not favorable to our social practice. But now, I will not care what others have to say. I do not care of their thoughts. I will only care for what matters to you. My greatest of friends, my pig Baconly.

Sir Alfred John

Sir Alfred John

Devotion

Michols' Herd

Memoirs of Sir Alfred John..........Cow Earsley

One day on my ranch, Cow Earsley and his companion wandered away from the herd to the northern side of the ranch. The hillsides to the north are full of trees and brush with small lakes wherever there is dip in any low land. At the same tyme, a small calf was heard crying in Lena's pond. The calf was stuck in the mud and slowly sinking. His head was leaning upward for survival. One of my most trusted ranch hands was nearby watching the event. Also watching was our most trusted family dog and fellow rancher, Michol,

The ranch hand had to make a quick distinct decision, to return the aged cows from the trees or save the small calf from drowning. With the hillside trees expected to slow the cow's adventure, he chose the latter.

He hurried and traveled his horse to the edge of the water, tied a rope to his horses' saddle and took the other end to the calf. Entering Lena's pond with the same difficulty as the calf, and getting bogged down in the mud, he finally reached to the calf and lassoed the rope safely around its neck. Swimming back to land, he led the horse by holding his reign and slapping his behind to get more plowing power. After many minutes, the calf was also lead out of the pond. The calf was exhausted and needed tending. So, the ranch hand nursed the calf with water and cleansed the thick mud from his hoofs. Not paying attention to tyme, but only the effort to save the calf, darkness started upon him. He knew that his return was eminent before a crew would be sent out to find him so he returned to the ranch, also knowing that the cows were no match for trees and brush. A return in the morning would find the cows since they were known not to stray.

The cattle ranch manager Norman congratulated his hand for making such a proper decision, as he was also confident that the two cows would be seen early in the morning. The cattle boss put together a search crew to find the cows. It started to snow heavily that morning so his crew thought to have the advantage of these cows not moving forward. Michol, the dog always participated in ranch activities and was again summoned to go with the search party. His strong sense of smell could only help them.

They searched for hours and hours. Finding no hoof marks or traces of broken branches all day, the crew was puzzled. They never lost cows in such a way. A second day search produced the same results. The third day produced the same. No more tyme could be spent on searching. Important winter preparation and chores were to near and falling behind. Therefore, I decided to discontinue the search.

Two weeks have past and snow is still on the ground. I was delivered another tragedy. Michol, my dog of German Shepherd decent, so skilled, and athletic, who could stand up straight, place his paws upon your shoulders and give you a human hug, was not seen since the day prior. He was a part of our family like even a son. This was not like Michol as a free running dog. He would stray for a short tyme, always returning within hours. The snow continuing to fall covered his tracks so we had no direction to search.

For the next few months when weather permitted, I sent out a ranch hand to look for the cows and Michol. I asked our traveling patrons and closest neighbors if they seen my strays and not a one found a sighting. My intuition became increasingly sad to the point of discontinuing the search. They were now either part of the wilderness, on my land or a neighboring property, or simply fell to this year's bad weather.

As the ground reappeared from the snow in the springtime, we now had to prepare the crops with seeding the dirt day after day. Rains were plenty for the plantation, filling the lakes and ponds and cleansing the hillsides. It was a good sign for the coming year's success.

This one-day however, was a different day. After nearly four months, a ranch hand screamed and shouted with excitement. "Everyone, come see, come see, on the hillside. Everyone, come quick, come see, look up there, Michol, Michol is coming."

We all looked up to the hillside, "My God," I shouted. "Everyone come see! Come see! It's Michol. He is leading the cows back to us. I cannot believe it. Look, there is also a new calf. I bet you that's why he could not return. The calf. He had to wait for spring so the calf could make the travel. Michol went to retrieve the cows. I bet he remembered the day they left and knew it was tyme for him to find them."

We all hurried and took our horses up the hillside to help Michol bring down the herd. His health and the herd he was guiding looked clean and well fed. It was as if Michol took care of them the same as his fellow human ranch hands would do. Feeling my spirit uplifted, I yelled out so loudly that it echoed across the hillside "Here comes Michol, a true rancher, a member of our family. He is truly loyal to the land. This is a great day for all of us. Let's celebrate!" And, celebrate, we did.

Sir Alfred John

Sir Alfred John

Foundation

Rosé Marie's Garden

Young and adventurous, aged at 17, was when Antonio first passed through my land. This year of our meet, Antonio was beginning his adult maturity, questioning life's path, and his future. Confused of his fate, he was looking for a beam of light to guide his destiny. Similar to what my youthful crossing into my manhood was, when it was my tyme to question. I suspect we all had to cross this line to maturity, prior to our doubt of life's future.

Planning his travels one-year prior, following in his directions, Antonio made passage through center of my land.

50

That one summer day, heading home for the early evening, I see Antonio seated on the Southside Bench located in RanchHands Field where visibility reaches across the worlds horizon, and its view enhances the mind to wander where the end of the world truly is. The bench is positioned on the highest hillside and has great views of fields where dreams excite the sense for travel upon it.

Southside Bench located in RanchHands Field sits alone on a pasture of rolling hills and its never ending fields seems to drop off beyond my earths view. This spectacular view of one bench, one man, one blueish cloudy sky overshadowing brownish green pasture below enhances my compassion for life, its adventure, and has the power to guide young aged men with life doubt, a route to follow, to find man he may become. For some, it can strike fear, for others, it provides an answer to a life quest. Only those brave and adventurous will bold themselves into it, just like Antonio, and will go beyond the horizon of the land, such as I, as my visions and dreams find tranquility and peace beyond the land.

As Antonio sat, staring into its depth, its passion, I remembered my time when my fate surrendered itself to the land, not the horizon. It was time for me to breath upon the land, discontinuing following the scent of the airs wind.

I commanded my horse Trotter to the bench so I may visit with Antonio. When I first arrived, we found quickly that we have many common interests; like farming, cooking, fencing, and making homemade wine. Missing dinner tyme, we talked extensively for hours late into evenings moon glow, sharing our life stories of family, our passions, our journeys, and our hardships.

Antonio was an explorer, his venturous soul guiding him. Antonio was out to find fun and adventure with hopes of finding a life partner to love, nurture, cherish, and to make family. However, a few weeks prior of his planned to find destiny Antonio fell upon, without spoken words, one person who made him gush with redness and a quivering of nervousness that he never felt before. He told me he was traveling to the north town to buy supplies for his farmland and he unexpectedly sidestepped a beautiful girl named Rosé Marie; who was tending her family's vegetable garden.

He met her as he walked by on the dirt road, chest high, showing a distinguished pride, he walked like a soldier in step, until embarrassing himself when he accidentally tripped his ankle off a small rock, falling face first directly onto her feet in the freshly churned garden soil. As she extended her arms to help him up and to balance his feet, their eyes glazed drawn together without blinking, as though the eyes were clinging onto each others thought of passion. The brief encounter was so short, but so breathtaking and memorizing, that he talked and laughed in stupidity as his tongue would twist his thoughts.

He was not at all confident that he made a favorable impression because when he spoke to her, his words were tongue tied. He would not tell me of their conversation, or what he said, but I suspect he knew it lacked logic.

He does tell me though his days of actual travel, his loneliness has grown more rapid, and his desire to take the planned travel weakens. Pondering his question himself of leaving what he left behind, on his own soil, meeting others in travel has become less intriguing.

At Southside bench, built on the high hilltop, Antonio took in its magic of the horizon and seeing its spirit, he could decided to no longer get her out of his heart. Every day, every moment, every time he looked beyond the horizon, the only earth he felt and sky he saw was his Rosé Marie.

As the evening expired, I invited Antonio to stay at the boarding house as a guest and in appreciation of my new friendship. He agreed.

The next morning, with little light of sun, Antonio placed his travel bag on his horse, with water, cooking supplies, shaving creme and a comb, to stop his northernly adventure to go back south, to what he now considered home.

As I wished him good health and a lifetime of happiness he said "thank you my good friend and your great vision of life, but it is today, from your lands horizon, that I make claim to true love placed into my heart, just a short tyme ago. I say to you Sir Alfred, goodbye and God bless. And, please, in my next travel, I will bring Rosé Marie to meet my new father figure of the north, and you and your family will see the passion of her loving heart."

He then boarded his horse and headed south, back home with a passion for Rosé Marie. A long eight days of hard travel.

Southside Bench, located on the high hilltop of RanchHands Field, placed another fine man destined to own the bearing fruits of this loving earth.

Sir Alfred John

Types of Vegetables

Legumes
- Beans; Black
- Beans; Broad
- Beans; Garbanzo
- Beans; Green
- Beans; Lima
- Beans; Pinto
- Beans; Snap
- Beans; Soy
- Beans; Wax
- Peas; Black
- Peas; Green

Root Vegetable
- Artichoke
- Beets
- Bok Choy
- Carrots
- Celery
- Chord; Swiss
- Fennel
- Onions; Boiling
- Onions; Garlic
- Onions; Green
- Onions; Leeks
- Onions; Scallion
- Onions; Shallots
- Onions; Spanish
- Onions; Sweet
- Onions; Yellow
- Parsnips
- Potato; Red
- Potato; Sweet
- Potato; White
- Radish
- Rutabaga

Leaf Vegetables
- Belgian Endive
- Butterhead
- Collard Green
- Iceberg
- Kale
- Mustard Green
- Romaine
- Sorrel
- Spinach
- Turnip Green
- Vine Leaves Cabbage
- Broccoli
- Brussels Sprout
- Cauliflower
- Green Cabbage
- Kohlrabi

Other Vegetables
- Asparagus
- Artichoke
- Bamboo Shoots
- Cardoon
- Celeriac
- Corn
- Fiddlehead
- Mushroom
- Parsnip

Cabbage
- Broccoli
- Brussels Sprout
- Cauliflower
- Green Cabbage
- Kohlrabi
- Red Cabbage
- Savoy Cabbage

Stalk Vegetable
- Bell Pepper
- Corn; White
- Corn; Yellow
- Cucumber
- Eggplant
- Okra
- Peppers; Green
- Peppers; Red
- Peppers; Yellow
- Peppers; Mild and Hot
- Pumpkin
- Squash; Acorn
- Squash; Buttercup
- Squash; Butternut
- Squash; Chayote
- Squash; Hubbard
- Squash; Pattypan
- Squash; Pumpkin
- Squash; Spaghetti
- Squash; Yellow
- Squash; Zucchini
- Tomato; Plum

Sir Alfred John

Fables

Piedo.... The Rabbit

Memoirs of Sir Alfred John..........The Tale of Friends

My daughter Romaine married my long tyme ranch manager Sir James Higgins, a thoughtful English gentleman in our employ for so many years. He told of daily dreams of someday taking stake in his own farm. A property he can call his homeland. With his hard-earned life savings, plus what I considered lucrative bonuses over the years, he purchased an exceptional rolling hills farming home. Now he could independently provide for his new wife and possible little Higgins children, my hopeful extension of family blood. Fortunately, for me, the land they chose was a local neighboring ranch distanced by one short county border reachable by horseback within less than one quarter-day travel.

Soon after they moved into their new homestead, days after the wedding, they were excited and very anxious to find new socials and trusting friends to spend fun days with. Seeing neighbors of same age they thought to find meaning to share a friendship. In their effort to demonstrate neighborly friendship they initiated costly concessions to the bordering property trying to show their regard for such picturesque views.

Together, in their first "married project", they removed dead trees and limbs, cut down high brush, repaired poor fencing, and removed debris from the former land owner. In a well thought out land strategy as well, the neighbors higher ground gave advantage to the land by providing vital rain water that fills their ponds and lakes. Any land owner of our tyme know fully that a neighborly dispute can ruin a ranchers passion. With their quest to please the lands borders would do much to not create dispute for nature's water rights.

The neighbor Sir Robert Fireman was known as a fair passionate man for his land and abundant crops, but was known more for his prize rabbit farm. He was the leader of county fair ribbons awards. One day, Sir Robert noticed Sir James working hard to the land and he invited him and wife Romaine to a private dinner. They accepted graciously.

Later in the evening, they strolled to Fireman's farm for their first meet. It was a delicious dinner of fresh plucked bird and vegetables, a most wonderful visit, just as they hoped for. They found each other shared common ideals, dreams, and the energy for life, and usually voiced accepted open debate on opposing political views. On this unique evening a special bond and friendship was borne.

Sir James and my daughter Romaine felt a reprieved from Fireman's neighborly acceptance, feeling now they could trust their new friends bond, whose overlooking view would help secure the land.

During their visit, they found entertainment in the Fireman family heartfelt discussion about raising home pets over the years which included dogs, cats, and rabbits. But, one particular pet was very dear to their hearts. It was a new born rabbit delivered as a wedding gift from Sir Willard's daughter Denise. It had a huge bounce of life in its step and was yet to be named. The day after he was gifted, thinking all day for his name, Sir Robert's wife Lady Norma Jean was preparing pie dough for that nights desert. Later that evening when the young curious rabbit was released out of his cage he ran instantly into the kitchen and leaped onto the flat rolled dough. Smashing into it, he stopped and took the largest baby bite possible in an attempt to fill out his little eight ounce frame. He then sat and lay directly onto the pie dough as though it was his sleeping blanket. With laughter erupting he created his own signature, they named him Piedo.

Sir James rabbits are always housed in a large penned cage located backside of the house, completely in view from the kitchen back window where Lady Norma enjoyed watching them run, jump, and play. Lady Norma Jean and Romaine soon gathered daily to socialize with tea, and then would venture to the pen to visit precious Piedo. With regular visits, Romaine grew attached to Piedo. He seemingly learned that his cuddliness fluffy fur and warm body could quickly gain friendship from those who dare place him close to their chest-heart. Feeling the pounding of his little heart beat, and comparing its timing to your own, you would also succumb to

Piedo. As months past the friendship grew with more socials and visitations.

One night my family needed to travel into town. We dropped our dog Michol to sit and board on Romaine's land. She loved Michol so much as she grew up with him usually playing all hours of the night. In this one late evening night everyone retired to bed and Michol took his position of sleep near the door where a blanket was in lay. As everyone adhered to the nights sleep, he would lay with head up, statue like, showing pride and respect understanding that his duty was to be our protector.

The following morning everyone woke to the early sunrise. Romaine looked out to pasture sighting Michol walking down the hillside toward the house. She shrieked a loud scream as she saw him carrying Piedo lightly between his jaws, seemingly displaying him as a trophy. Romaine said with great fear,

"Oh Piedo, Oh no, it's Piedo. What are you doing Michol! My Dear God, what has he done?

Realizing her panic made her voice loud she concentrated on keeping it in control so not to notify the Fireman's. Seeing her dear friend Piedo stilled in the Michol's mouth she determined immediately that Michol must of accidentally killed Piedo.

Sir James hearing the commotion ran fearlessly into the kitchen. Both now seeing what looked like a fresh kill, were astonished and angered by the sight.

They did not know immediately what to do so stood silently in disbelief and displeasure. After a few moments their minds settled. They looked at each other knowing that this would destroy any hope of continuing their neighborly friendship.

Michol finally entered the kitchen and laid Piedo to the feet of Lady Norma. She cried. She then ran Michol out the door and shut it with anger. She was confused trying to make sense of the whole situation.

Hours later, they began to discuss ways to tell Sir Roberts family of their hardship. They finally thought to directly face the Fireman's eye directly at their front door as this would suggest good strong character. With both in agreement this was the only civilized plan as their pride could not face being silent. In the next early morning, they began the dreadful walk uphill to cross the neighbors' border, knowing there was no return. They sadly carried Piedo in hand ready to face whatever punishment would come about them. It was risky to admit the dogs kill but they needed to keep the water flow running downstream.

As they crossed the border line their hearts dropped further into guilt. A few meters onto the land they saw the entire Sir Higgins family leaving the farm by horse and carriage. First confused, together they realized the opportunity to get out of the whole situation. But, this was riskier than before and would go against them if the get caught. Looking at each other in an unspoken agreement they quickly ran upward to the pen. Once there, they both said, "help me God" and tossed Piedo over the pens fence onto the open dirt floor. The plan was simple, If only the neighbors would first find Piedo lying in the pen, they would conclude that prey attacked inside its cage. No suspicion would arise, no blame for

Michol. In nervousness, they tossed Piedo over the fence and immediately turned down the hill running full speed back to the house.

For a couple weeks thereafter there was no neighborly interaction. This was unusual for such good friends. Each day, as the silence gave them doubt of success, Sir James and Romaine continued a heated discussion of what they did. More bothersome was throwing Piedo back without a proper burial. They felt small and low in character. Now, they surely could not face Sir Robert with the truth.

Finally, one cloudy day, looking every day through the window they saw both Sir Robert and Lady Norma Jean walking down to their farm. Both Higgins nerves started to chatter as their mind now wondered what to do and how to interact.

The door knocked, seemingly louder that ever heard before. They opened the door together unknowing what they were about to face.

They said in a confused voice "How are you today, dear Robert and Norma?

Sir Robert replied with the deepest of voice never heard before.

He said, "Dear Sir, I must tell you of a neighborly problem we have".

Sir James and Romaine hearts fell to the ground and their faces flushed a near pinkish color. In their guilty minds, they were ready for punishment,

Sir Robert continued saying, "I found Piedo lying awkwardly on the rabbit pens door. He was dead!"

Sir James heart started racing rapidly as he fluttered each outgoing word into a scramble. He could not breath to speak. Glancing nervously at each other for support they knew to tell the truth and beg desperately hoping for mercy but this was sure to damage their neighborly trust.

With Sir James's seemingly sputtering words of boredom, long delay, Sir Robert saw an opportunity to speak over him.

With exuberance in his low voice, he said "I been wanting to visit for the last couple weeks to caution you of deep concern of ours. We believe someone passed onto our farm and believe this person to be dangerous! He might just be crazy!"

With a confused look, Sir James lifted his head in surprise and let him continue.

"Sir James, let me tell you what dreadful thing happened a couple of weeks back. We found our lovely Piedo in the late evening laying on the ground with natural death. Our family then buried him a proper grave and thought to go into town the following morning to get ribbon for the wooden cross we placed. When we came back from town, we found Piedo's grave scattered and empty. Looking around we found him lying awkwardly on his pens ground. Would you believe that someone dug Piedo out of his rock covered grave and threw him back into his pen? What strange man would do such a thing?"

"I want to warn you of this person because he must be of evil thought and may pass on your land as well. Please keep a sharp eye on anyone you see in this area that looks primitive as he."

Without thought Sir James and Romaine were relieved. They escaped charges of idiocy and found relief that Michol was not a the killer. Sir James quickly thanked Sir Robert in half-wit broken sentences of garbled words; letting him know of the appreciation.

But then, Sir Robert in a very unusual manner, turned quickly with upbeat speed to return uphill to his farm. Simply saying, "I must go now and will see both of you again"

With this unusual closure of Sir Robert, Sir James and Romaine started having thoughts of what just happened and hid in home that night, continuing discussions about the strange behavior they just witnessed. With both now in doubt of which story is truth, Romaine asked Sir James "did Sir Robert know of their direct involvement and decided to save our friendship by white lying, or did he truly believe a man passed through the land."

Years later, the unknowing of truth left both feeling in doubt to the point of confusion. But, one thing is certain, this fact will never be spoken of again......either by the Higgins family or the Fireman family. That is because whatever is the truth, today they are still great friends and even greater companions. They simply know that sometimes things are just best left to never be told.

Sir Alfred John

Sir Alfred John

Dreams

The Fish that Ate My Mother!

Memoirs of Sir Alfred John..........Mom's Favorite Date

In a day long ago my mother Anna Rosé made her first fishing trip. She was aged twenty-nine, so she says. Her husband, Sir Raymond, a hard working farming person, motivated by their love of six year marriage created a family of three sons. Their goal was simple, spend more time together. With Raymond being a avid fisherman and going alone too often, he decided to ask her if she would go along with him into the ponds. He thought catching a fresh fish dinner would get her interested and maybe spend more tyme with her in his sport.

My mother, a very petite woman with little girly charm, standing less than five foot tall, and weighing merely ninety-eight pounds, also wanted to be more active with Sir Raymond's sport. They both wanted this time together. With so many years that she was not invited to these ponds she accepted excitingly but with nervous anticipation.

The night before the pond, mother kept from sleeping for most of the night fearful of what creatures would come from the ponds. When she was able to sleep, her unconscious dreams would show a barbarous creature, large in shape with long sharp yellowish teeth inside a moving jaw, looking to bite often. As the night wore on the dreams intensified depriving her of a rest.

Mother considered telling him of these dreams but felt he would never invite her again. So she kept her fear quietly inside, hidden in her heart.

On this sunshiny Saturday, Sir Raymond and Anna Rosé headed to Lena's pond with a filled picnic basket of food, wine, and candles, along with plenty of gear to make evenings fish dinner a reality.

Both arriving on tyme to Lena's pond, Sir Raymond was anxious to enjoy the day of fishing and very eager for the relaxation of the hunt.

The picnic blanket was laid evenly across the grass and them upon it. Sir Raymond, an experienced fishing kind, prepared the fishing pole for her, as a manly gesture to a women. He tied a hook and weighted it to the end of the line. He then placed a live lured worm onto it. Mother seeing this closed her eyes half way in disgust while the other half watched in curiosity. Her hunting tool was now ready. This was all so primitive to her.

As Sir Raymond handed over the fishing pole, unaware of last night nightmares, he said "this little worm can catch the largest of fish and if you do, you can win a prize from the community, but you must bring it onto the land." This comment reinforced her dreams that there was something larger that life that lived in the water. Why would there be larger fish than caught before, she wondered.

After a moment or so, she then summoned her courage back to fish with Sir Raymond on the shore. After all this was what she wanted, to be part of his sport life, to be together.

They arrived near the waters bank. She took her pole and made her first ever attempt to launch, but the line landed short, only a meter hitting the ground. Her second toss would only go a few meters, but at least now hitting the waters edge. She casted again and again with mixed results none that would catch fish.

Sir Raymond looked at her with confusion and realized this is going to be a rough day but collecting his thoughts he remembered in his youth when he casted the same prior to training. So he shrugged off her casts and reinsured her that the next one would be more rewarding. He showed her techniques in hope to gain her confidence and see a successful launch. He knew with just one good long toss, it would be a better day, since he decided that it could sit in the water for hours and hours at a tyme.

Now prepared with training, mother eagerly reeled the pole behind her and without regret released the weighted hook into a high arc that fell a good depth into the water. Excited and proud by the success of this launch, she looked at Sir Raymond and said proudly, "I told you I can do this" as though she just became a social member of the mens angler society.

Only a few minutes after launch though, a sudden yank prevailed the line, bending the poles tip to the water, wiggling it violently. Mother never seen such as thing.

Sir Raymond excitingly told her "you caught a fish, you caught a fish, now bring it to shore, reel it in, bring it to shore!" Well mother never heard reel it in. Feeling the line tighten and wiggle she now felt in her hand what her mind was showing. The night monster thrashed back into her thoughts. Immediately she sent signals of fear. A high screeching non ending pitch of sound bellowed out from her internal body as thought the lungs were as large as her.

When Sir Raymond saw her face turn bloodless white she took her body about face and immediately ran towards the most safe place, the cabin. But, as she ran she forgot to let go of the pole.

She ran and ran and ran, at least two hundred yards to the porch. Sir Raymond followed quickly as best he could but was slowed with his self inflicted belly laugh that started when he saw her eye fear up to the biggest of circles. His run to catch her was no match for her screaming speed. Moments later, as he finally reached porch, his belly laugh deepened uncontrollably. It would not quit.

What he saw lay there on the porch floor was a very little confused and exhausted five-inch baby pan fish, looking more scared by its recent flight of being bounced across the earth's rocky floor which is not as fluid as what water use to provide. He then saw her white ghost face looking at the flapping green monster, dropping the pole, and again running to where ever she thought would be more safe.

He could not stop laughing for days on end.

She would never fish again!

Sir Alfred John

Sir Alfred John

Friendship

Antonio's Legacy

A Story in the Life of Sir Alfred John..........The BlackRose

Passionate of life, culture and adventure, young lovers, Antonio and Rosé Marie, always dreamed of exploring the world together leaving behind their Italian homeland. Antonio began this endeavor of learning about cultural ethnicity when he learned of a safe stay and travel passage through the ranchland of Sir Alfred John, a prominent horse trader of England.

When Antonio first arrived at the ranch shortly after sunrise, Sir Alfred John seated him to an old wooden hand built oak welcoming table, and ordered him and Antonio a complimentary elegant French wine. As always, Sir Alfred John joined him with great interest and curiosity. As they talked, they soon discovered many common interests including farming, cooking, and making homemade wines. They talked extensively sharing stories of their life's experiences and  hardships. Trusting their new found friendship, Antonio shared his most heartfelt tragedy. You see Antonio's anguish began after his beloved wife Rosé Marie passed from illness. Rosé Marie and Antonio's dream would never be. Rosé Marie made Antonio promise her that he would take their journey of travel northward with eyes wide open and she in his heart. Thus she too would see the world through his eyes, and be with him in every step he takes in life. Shortly thereafter her death, Antonio sold their home and belongings, secured passage northeastward to England through the ports in Calais, France. He headed with horseback passing through London, Colchester, Ipswich to Norwich where he was resting before traveling to his final destination of Manchester, England.

Sir Alfred John invited Antonio to dinner that evening to  impress him with his cooking but Antonio agreed only if he could prepare the dish. Sir Alfred John agreed and provided the pork whilst Antonio ventured thru Sir Alfred's garden, picking its fresh vegetables. Antonio impressed by the enriched garden selection of herbs and vegetables, selected the best of its sweet peppers and most pungent of fresh herbs. Sir Alfred John looked on privately while Antonio prepared the meal. He saw Antonio reaching into his travel bag and pulled out his own traveled treasure of herbs. He mixed the ingredients together, dipped the pork into it, and set it to the side allowing the meat to absorb all its wonderful flavours.

Sir Alfred John impressed with Antonio's dish, asked Antonio if he could add it to his signature recipes collection. Antonio hesitating his request but only a few seconds, in a gesture of excitement and trust of their relationship, Antonio replied "I would be glad to do so under one important personal lifetime commitment". Sir Alfred John, puzzled by the reaction, asked, "Mr. Antonio, my friend, what is the demand you seek so persistently for?"

Antonio replied, "With my utmost respect of you and your fine land as shown through your garden dear Sir, and as my new and trusted friend, I request your calling of this fine recipe be named as Black Rosé."

Sir Alfred John, curious of Antonio's strongest language so far, asked, "Why is it your desire for such a name". Antonio replied, "You see Dear Sir, the day Rosé Marie passed, it was the blackest day in my lifetime. I lost my best friend, my most loyal companion, and my heart. This recipe was Rosé Marie's best creation. It is for her, all of her passion and heart for flavor in life is expressed through this perfect blend of our earth's creations."

"My Rosé Marie fed me this very flavorful dish in our first dinner together, as her intent was to impress me with what future dinners could be. And, with acquiesce of our hearts from that day to now, my one love and my only daily thought, is Rosé Maria. She would serve me this dish regularly to remind me of the beautiful memory of that day and each beautiful day that followed."

"I had a black day in my life, the passing my Rosé Marie, but all the other days of our lives were of sweetest of loves and friendships. So, by you giving this blend the name Black Rosé and passing it onto all the travelers staying or passing through your land, my Rosé Marie in some way also pass her heart onto others. I would like them to feel her passion."

"Moreover, with you agreeing to pass the story of my family to who desires to hear it, dear Sir, I would be honored for you to speak it as your own Black Rosé."

With Great Respect of Antonio and Rosé Marie,

And also with your loss,
may your heart keep their spirit true.
Michael, the Author

Sir Alfred John

Learnt

Influence

Fathers before me taught culinary with placing their pens-hand onto cloth paper to record their findings. They forwarded our society with experimentations of flavoured plant use same as discovering medical plants that help cure. We have learnt far more in our tyme than older tymes before about food survival, storage, and distribution. My thoughts wander on how these forefathers maintained food survival without our modern salt preservation and cool storages. My inquisitiveness lead me to buggy Edward Thomas Boardman at his library in Norwich downtown to discuss such curiousness.

Centuries prior to our pre-settled England, field grains and corn,freshly speared fish and primitive day animal hunts provided mankind with its daily nutritional energy. In a all day hunt for free running red-blood animal were mans daily task. Although herds were more abundant than this day, animal was not restricted by our territorial stone hedges, which made hunt travel to reach tiring miles.

The work ritual of this mans animal hunt was tasked by tribal groups. Group members were those who trusted each other, not always immediate family. When the hunt begun in early morn the women homesteaded and readied the fire pit with baked grain and heated river water, so to make animal blood gravy upon the return of a fresh kill day. When the hunt failed to provide red meat, wild hens, or fish, the group ate strictly on the prepared grain of oats and barley, and waited for the next days hunt. With many days of unsuccessful hunt, small game like rabbit and plucked bird along with flavourful plant weeds would substituted the missing kill. Finding its way into the boiling pot provided thicker than water flavour.

When week long hunts failed the hunter and meat starvation prolonged, the hunter took upon his tribal pride to eat until large kills fell upon them. They do this for the sake of family first, even if they sicken themselves, lost energy, and died. In this tribal ritual, it seemingly was self weakening and almost sure death not to eat prior to the hunts.

I always think of this tribe when my day to day trials of hard life do not bring my light and I realize the sanctimony and enjoyment of being socially educated , a practitioner in trade, and moreover, knowing that a stone hedged land allows me to eat.

Sir Alfred John

Sir Alfred John

Patrimony

Learn Sausage, Learn Culinary

Memoirs of Sir Alfred John..........Create Your Own

Sausage has a persons special flavour character stamped into it when created from a culinary passion. Each recipe finds its unique personal taste created only by the artist performing the mix. The blending of meat, oil, fat, and spice is truly a sausage making art and a great way to learn the art of culinary.

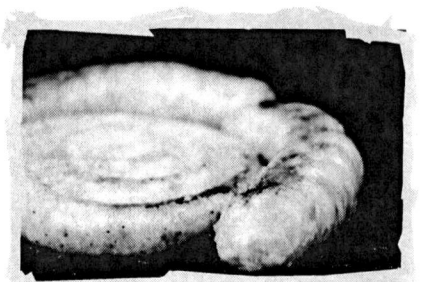

I learned the lesson of sausage making when I was very young. I visited the towns meat market regularly to see proprietors Sir Willard making homemade sausages. The Italian was was the most flavourful and delicious of all the links. I had a passionate desire to duplicate this tasty sausage and maybe with luck, make it even better. Setting out to my self-challenge, I traveled back and forth many tymes to watch and learn Sir Willard's craft whilst looking at other shelves of shopping interest. I would purchase some to dissect it, first peeling off its skin and surgically separating its ingredients visibly under a fine reading magnifier. With vigorous trial and error, I repeated my dissection over and over in attempt to determine its ingredients.

But after two years of having no success of duplication, I finally gave up to claim the recipe impossible. I then decided to confront Sir Willard of the next tyme I was in town to speak openly about his recipe. Weeks later I entered the market, looked directly into his eyes and asked Sir Willard if he would share his recipe with me. In a loud voice, he declined. Not what I expected. But in his response I learnt the most important culinary rule.

He told me in a angered but also passionate voice, "Dear young John, you are not the first, nor the last in the endeavor to duplicate my sausage flavour. I am an experienced sausage maker of whom over many personal attempts developed my

sausage. To duplicate my s ausage flavour you must possess the same ingredients mixed only as I do. Then I sized the sausage in my desire way and called it mine, a personal trademark to me. Young John this sausage is my creation, not yours or any other persons. It is made perfectly for my pallet and I only wish to share its final mix within a sealed skin. I prepare this by my own hand so it's creation is special to me, and me alone."

"I know why you and others visit my market. You come to smell the aroma of flavour and to watch my sausage making so to learn from your visits. You constantly view my butchering table to get a glimpse of what meats and spices I may use. As I watched you watching me, I knew you were trying to steal my recipe because you would always leave without a single purchase. Believe me, there have been many before you who have done the same. For those prior to you and those whom come after you, I will always say the same. Your creation is yours, my creation is mine. And what flavour is personally yours you would not want me to duplicate either.

Simply stated my boy, this is the truth about culinary; your creation is yours and yours alone."

Always remember this young John....flavour is held by the hand which measures it, so be creative with the spice."

While receiving this scolding, my heart weighted deep into my stomach, my face flushed of embarrassment, and my ears opened to attention. I took deep breaths in an attempt to recover my skin back to its original color but it took some tyme.

After my nerves settled, I finally realized my fruitless attempts of curiosity was really a passion for the culinary. I didn't understand this until I received his scolding. One of Sir Willard's unknown greatest achievements is the passion that he gave onto me.

He taught me that ingredients can only be molded into perfection by efforts of the originator and with my sausage duplication attempts, I failed to be the originator. I now realize by making a truly honest effort to perfect my own recipe, I can then make claim to it.

As an adult now thinking of that day, I now thank Sir Willard for teaching me the rule of culinary. Looking back on that day of total embarrassment, I now laugh because not only did I leave the store with a new vision, I left penny-less after over-purchasing three months supply of his fine sausage.

Sir Alfred John

Sir Alfred John

Comfort

Family Tradition

Memoirs of Sir Alfred John..........Comfort Food

I write my diary today to reflect on our family tradition.

Land and animal work is hard. It is hard for everyone; the ranch hands, the family, the pets, and as well wears on the animals and plants of the land.

When rains do not come, I see stress creeping from brown thirsty grasslands, fish straining in ponds with low water levels, and the hot baking sun wilting the exposed plant life. On these long days, I see dehydration from our skin when the sun evaporates moisture from it.

To provide us rest from the suns wear, trees provide a place to rest and to cool. The lakes provide drink, and the swim thereafter cools and cleans us. However, what I find most resting is the return home to my loving wife Joyce, who patiently waits for our return to serve us her fabulous meatloaf.

Her servings are always plentiful and delicious every tyme she makes it. We know when she makes it when the pungent of aromas covers the ranch air as so to call us home for needed rest. Through our years of her serving this dish, it continues to call us together as a family, and resembles our life, and our love for each other, and our family.

She brings the family together with this meal. It keeps us close and in comfort to know that she will always be there for us and always love us. Therefore, I declare this dish to be our family's tradition.

Sir Alfred John

Sir Alfred John

Innovation

Popcorn Turkey

Memoirs of Sir Alfred John..........Chef Sir Norman

Our rolling fields are filled with corn stalks with naturally  grown protective husks covering the corn kernels in hopes of securing them from passing birds. As we have been in drought this year each day the corn stalk yearns for its next rainfall to get its drink. In these fields, commonly running wild turkey would pass at its base hiding to avoid the hunting fox. They were plentiful.

In the past couple weeks we have had hard cattle drives. So on this Sunday we elected to have a festive ranch hands rest day. Our lead ranch hand for cattle drives was Norman and he is always excited for the tyme off. He decided to fetch a few Wild Turkeys and cook it for that evening's ranch hands dinner. What a treat when cattle boss Norman cooks! When he does everyone will venture to come.

Norman, a simplistic average man grew to position by hard work and love for the travel across the land. His skills of cattle for cash trading are exceptional as he seems to always get top dollar. He is one truly dedicated to the work of the land. Known to pull off quite delicious party feasts on numerous drives, he pleased mans hunger with imaginative servings, not at all tentative in his flavorings. In this regard, the crew members looked forward to his preparation knowing dinner would be made with Norman pride.

Early in the morning, Norman took to the hunt to get his birds. Calling on our dog Michol for side assist, they took to the fields. Within only hours they proudly returned carrying three turkey birds on the backside of the cargo horse, along with an abundant amount of corn. He thought to not pick the younger fresh corn harvest not so ready, so he picked up the recent fallen, which was nearly dry due to the drought.

Sir Norman prepared the birds by beheading the necks, plucking their feathers, and cleansing the cavities. With open cavity, they were now primed for succulent corn dressing.

On this day of creation, with his newest thought, he peeled the corn from the tusks, mixed it with oil, water, and seasoning expecting it to soften the kernel into a fine tasting corn pudding.

To prepare the bird, he placed large Great Sea salt pellets, coloured peppers and plant herbs over and under the bird's skin to meld into the meats flavouring.

The cast iron kettle was placed above a pre-heated wood flame and Norman coated the iron with a small amount of oil and water to cover the pans bottom so to steam the bird and stuffing. Now with a fair high heat he placed the turkeys into the kettle with tails upward, weighing the bird down tightly with the cast iron cover. It was now tyme to wait the cook.

During the day, he would brag to those who didn't witness his preparation to get their tongues and imagination into pre-taste. He had a habit of doing this in attempt to make less desirable food blunders taste better then they should. Everyone with great imagination was now anxious to have a great dinner sooner than later.

Later on, now getting near to the end of the birds tenderness, a wonderful smell signaled the crew across the area. As the smell grew more pungent, more crew gathered to help finish.

As the crew stood circled around the kettle with drink pleasures in hand, talking of old stories and adventure, a crackling noise was heard in the kettle. It sounded like the cast metal was to split. As the noise became more rapid, no one trusted the metal to hold the turkeys if it split. Everyone discussed if they should remove it from the heat but also knew dinner tyme was to be soon. So it was decided to let it cook. As they wait, the popping noise increased to a musical instrument, similar to a drum. Within moments of this sound, seemingly seconds of tyme, the kettle cover exploded loudly. It flew straight up into the air flying above the fire pit and landed near a rancher feet. Everyone started laughing loudly with exuberance.

Following immediately was an abundance of cooked popcorn tossed into the air like a tornado of debris, spitting white popcorn from the rear cavities of the birds, shooting Norman and those who would dare stare at it, similar as a shoot of shrapnel from a cannon.

One crewman laughing uncontrollably, spoke out, "this turkey had one more thing to say about us in life. Norman you must of really made this bird angry at us for ending his tyme because as you see, he revenged himself upon us!"

Everyone present burst into a loud uncontrolled belly laugh laughter, knowing that this moment was Norman's best blundered creation.

Norman, completely embarrassed, needing his fulfill his cattle trail dinner legacy, attempted to cover up his mistake by saying with head held high pride,

"Gentleman, what you witnessed is my version of Popcorn Turkey Stuffing. A delicate light side dish to our turkey meal today, would you all please help me pick it up and place it properly in your dish? I will begin to serve the bird. Thank you!"

Everyone knowing Norman's the boss, laughed for hours, but did pick up what they could.

Sir Alfred John

Sir Alfred John

Prestige

Cattleman's Pride

Memoirs of Sir Alfred John..........Competitive Cows

Beef burger is amongst controversy within our cooking socials. It is a ranchers signature.

Good tasting beef chuck shredded and packed that we call hamburger. Feeding cattle on one land and the same species on another man's land can have beef taste so differently, and so unique to ones land they occupy. Why does one come out moister and some less tender. Why does beef taste so opposite from each cattle borne?

Our cattle feed upon the regions freshest most nutritional of lands, eating plentiful tall grass that grows quickly within our rich soil. They drink from natural waters of our many springs and rain ponds, free running rivers and blue clear lakes. Nevertheless, continuous from one landowner to another we all have made our shredded beef unique to our lands taste. In our region, the flavour of shredded beef seems to symbolize each landowner's portrayal of his hard work on his unique land and a statement of his character.

I, of course, believe that my beef is the best of all shredded beefs because of my lands care and location, plus adding of my beef spice, and my most secret ingredient, a dash of milk cream. With the spice and milk cream combination high flame will not so quickly dry the meat center, avoiding toughening and doneness. The meat seals and the milk cream melds the burger patty's internal flavour, prolonging its moistness.

I must say that I do give complements to others, as this represents their unique beef burger and provides characterization of themselves. I do however find that I best enjoy more of the compliments coming toward me.

After all, I favor my land over any other.

Sir Alfred John

Sir Alfred John

Pursuit

Fish Bugs

Today, my longtime friend Captain John Seaman went to catch delicate fish and seafood. I knew he would since it is the first Friday of the month when he would pleasure himself with a private fishing trip along the rivers channel of the North Sea. He was rigidly predictable in this way.

I decided to travel into the harbor to trade him with his favorite fresh quality beef, brain, and tongue, for his least favorite and my most desirable sea shrimp. After all, I have too much beef and it would spoil in a few weeks since travelers would slow in the winter weather. I prepared the beef in sea salt and burlap wraps many tymes keep it moist and cool for its coming travel. I did not want the sun to spoil it. Today I was extra hungry for any type of seafood catch because I have not shared its taste for some tyme now.

108

I started travel in the morning and I arrived at the harbor three hours before nightfall expecting Captain John to enter the port at any tyme! As I said, he is rigidly predictable in this way. Others townsmen and fellow travelers would arrive the same, as they knew that Captain John and other fisherman would trade for whiskey, staples, crafts, and the exchange of our great English pound.

This day though, Captain John did not arrive back at the usual hour. Most of us waited and waited, hours passed and it was near dark with the sun half-sunken in the water. When on the horizon, we saw a fishing ship. It was Captain John. As he drew near, those who remained gathered round to help him moor his boat to the harbor poles.

Now tied and secure, we came to the edge of the deck to enter but could not. We all gasped at the sight of what would be Captain John's most spectacular catch of his lifetime. The decks color was darkened with so many shrimp that it covered the boat from stem to stern. The shrimp ran freely on top of each other trying to reach the seawater puddles upon the deck. Their flight was everywhere, including any hole into the lower storage and sleeping areas.

The Harbormaster shouted aloud, "Captain John, we worried with fear you may have been troubled with waters. Why did you return home so close into the night?"

Captain John spotted me in the crowd. He shouted "Dear Sir Alfred John, my friend, I have a slight problem. My crew and I caught so many shrimp in one load that I could not place my net in the cargo area to store my load. We are stuck here and can't walk towards you for every tyme we do these little fish bugs get in the way. Would you help us gain a path so we can get off my ship?"

I responded "Dear Captain John Sir, what happened? Why are the shrimp swimming freely on your deck."

Captain John replied. "This morning we lowered the net to the sea floor since the waters were calm. After many hours of giving our tongue the pleasure of Molly's fine drink and when realized the thought of it tyme to lift we realized our stay was much too long. Somehow, the ship accidentally floated to a rivers rock edge and secured itself. We tried to lift the net but it seemed weighted with rock or stuck on the edge. So we moved the boat to release the net."

"As we lifted the net quickly, the weight lowered our starboard into the water and took on some sea. I thought we were going over but we worked to balance the ship with placing and weighted article to the port side. It took all five of us to lift the net with the lift beam bending like a tree. I was sure to losing the net and the beam to the water if we moved to suddenly. We dragged on so not to lose the net of what we thought of as rocks and fish. As the net neared the surface, we saw these huge black moving shadows within the net so we thought to have a heavy load of heavy rock, fish, and shrimp."

When the crew saw that, the net was full of the bug sea creatures they began to work harder to bring them to surface. I don't know why they like these bugs. But, if they like these bugs then that is what we will do. Bring them aboard.

The net was so weighted and full that it took us long to bring the bug herd over the deck to nearly the cargo entry. But, as the net got over the boat, the lift pole splintered in two and dropped these bug creatures on our heads. My ship and I are going to smell just like a sea bug for many weeks to come. I guess I will not be welcome at anyone social for a while. I will not smell like a man for some tyme to come.

As he realized that his favorite occasion is socials and they may have now been jeopardized to this most ridiculous notion of smelling like a shrimp, he angrily called out, "Please, everyone take these bugs; take them freely off my boat. In trade, I would request your service to help clean my boat tomorrow. That evening with the rapidly spreading event reaching town, it triggered off a thunder of excitement and later, fun and entertainment. Looking up the dirt road heading into the harbor I saw the dirt road filling with townspeople to collect what they could of the free offering of shrimp. They brought kettle pots, firewood, and pits for its cooking, plus more of Molly's drink to assist in their socializing. The gathering went on and on to the morning with dance and music.

The next day, Captain John's boat became clean as the last few citizens searched and took home all the left over shrimp on the ship.

Sir Alfred John

112

REFERENCES:
www.oldukphotos.com/suffolk-lowestoft.htm

Sir Alfred John

Recollection

Rock Shrimp

Memoirs of Sir Alfred John.........A Later Entry

I remember how we all laughed that day of the shrimp catch festival and how we still laugh in these months after Captain John's episode. More than ever how on that weekend, how the whole town came to eat on his Bug Shrimp catch. We joke in taverns and in social visits to friends about Captain Johns exciting way to tell us his story that when we cook shrimp we call it "Bug Shrimp". However, with trade down in following season, the local town's officials proclaimed to marketers that the name "bug shrimp" was not in the town's best interest when at market so they proclaimed that the fishing communities call them "Rock Shrimp".

The name stuck with the fishing vessels, the harbors, and the fresh fish market, but for those of us who witnessed this eventful day, we, with great respect, will privately call it "Bug Shrimp".

Sir Alfred John

Sir Alfred John

Apportion

Port of Call

Memoirs of Sir Alfred John.........Markets of Distribution

As a very young boy growing up in England's vast and growing society, I would visit the Great Sea to smell its salt air and view of the large cargo ships passing or entering port. Knowingly that each ship was loaded with worldly ingredients of newly cut spices, delicate fruits, or freshly caught sea fish, I would imagine its worldly journey. The flowing air breezed across the ocean water passing the ships scent onto land sending a signal to all the townspeople that trade was about to take place. Without doubt, the scent lured buyers to the pungency of its smell, to venture its new findings of familiar and not so familiar cargo. After all, buying direct from sea Captains cost pennies less than stockiest merchants, and as bonus, it was free of taxation.

For such a tyme, so many new plants, spices and herbs were coming to us from all over the newly explored world, spreading sensation and excitement to our tasting pallets, that we could only imagine how to place it into an evening dish. Duplicating an aspiration was usually simple, but if it did not flavour as the imagined meal would taste in our minds then our family always consider it a good flavoured dish because of our family valued our entertainment whilst being together.

In later years however, over tyme, with any abound commodity, distribution and trade became more sophisticated and costly. Supply was stretching into other ports and harbors and the high demand found political pressure for

this importation of plants to be taxed. As politicians changed laws to make revenue for the town, we could purchase sea merchants cargo directly as they tied to dock, but prices were raised to the demand of government seemingly to protect the profits of merchant stockiest and retailed business. Direct cargo ships no longer offered advantage except for freshness of catch.

During this same tyme of political intrusion, our farming economy slipped from an unusual cold climate that damaged much of the vegetation. The once standing lines of dock customers reduced to only few which were those whom had a profitable animal crop. Which continued to lessen in numbers as the fields dried that year. This economic downturn together with taxes and worldwide demand wanting our ship staples, the price of commodities, the favorite plant spices, fruits, nuts, and herbs, simply became an unaffordable extravagance. Out of need of our commoners still wanting its flavour advantage, a black market was born.

Local hired common men were hired for their hands to be ship cleaners. To make their penny paid job more lucrative they would take bottom ship scraps into the streets were you could sell secretively on the black market, in back cornered alleys, where dim light exists. When police were distracted by an emergency or when dark cloud, night, or rainfall could provide cover, the smallest volume of cargo commodities were sold to the highest bidder. It is said buy anything in these streets if you were willing to pay its price. At that tyme, the smell of aged cargo was a delight because the price of nothing was worthless.

On this day with elders living in a more progressively learnt society and somewhat wiser than youth, we admit our economy and sustaining jobs rely on active trade through a multi-tier distribution. Sanctioning illegal trade acts and our changing political attitude towards our economic stimulus, politicians eased up on taxation fees that allowed balance between consumers and merchants alike. Improving distribution, our stockiest supported filling their shelves with great pleasure, strengthening economy...........along with my wealth.

Sir Alfred John

Sir Alfred John

Consumption

The Blue

Memoirs of Sir Alfred John..........The Great Light Blue

The town council has built a new blubber oil lighthouse so to attract passing trade ships to port. Blue whale blubber has become such an important staple lighting our street and our homesteads darkest corners. This new lighthouse rests its flickering sunlight across the oceans surface in search of men seeking the pleasure of land. Such a great light, its yellowish orange campfire brightness cannot be avoided. Once on land, the great light directs our activities to our nightly socials and events. Our great friendships can last into the moonless night and provide our carriages direction back late in the evening.

Thank God for the Blue Whale. Its amputation of fat is a god send.

Sir Alfred John

The Blue

Memoirs of Sir Alfred John..........My First Blue

I witnessed my first blue today as it came to port hauled in by a large scrimshaw fishing vessel. I've hear these great sea captain's trade town merchants its whale sperm and fat blubber for food and supplies so they can continue travel.What a spectacular magnified creature when stills tied to the ships port. They are so magnificent with its richness in deep blue and under-carriage of vanilla white, so deep of blue that it reflects a haze of shininess; and oh, so large! How do these mammals get so large? How much do they feed? What in Gods creative pack of great balance in predators could match such a massive belle on? What in the great sea must they pleasure their daily intake in order to survive its size?

Sir Alfred John

Sir Alfred John

Annihilate

The Blue

Memoirs of Sir Alfred John..........Blue Whaling Ships

I see blue whale regularly every day when in town. Sometimes two to three tied to the ships drag. I remember seeing one as a child when the blues were treated as a majestic mammal of our seas. Hundreds of blue enter port each month now. With so many whaling ships coming and going, in and out of port, back and forth, are the seas straining from overuse? Will they be plentiful in our future?

We kill blue for our survival. Is their population so plentiful that they can continue to light our towns, our neighbors town, their neighbor? The world? Are their populations declining so rapidly that their destiny is extinction? Oh God, I hope not. I would condemn myself if I would see this come to pass during my days on this earth. Our humanity must find a way to change our lamp methods so we can stop this obstrocity. I wonder what can be done?

Sir Alfred John

The Blue

Facts About Blue, the Authors Perspective..........The Last Blues
The Truth About Blue Whale Population

According to the Canadian Museum of Nature, 30,000 blue whales were slaughtered in one year alone, it was 1931. In the year 2000, there were only 10,000 blues remaining worldwide. Blues grow to 100 feet long and can weigh up to 150 tons. Its heart is the size of a small calf. If the slaughter was for oil lamps and the manufacturing of soap, have we learned from this early event that natural gas will have a similar fate? In so many ways, one thing we know is history will always repeat itself.

REFERENCES:
http://www.nature.ca/notebooks/english/bluwale.htm

Sir Alfred John

Legacy

Olde Tyme Wood Cooking

Memoirs of Sir Alfred John..........Pit Cooks Heritage

Why must we lose our traditions in cooking barbecue? Who introduced this sauce to our barbecue to ruin our meat flavour? What is this newer tomato red-based barbecue paste that is being applied to the smoking pit meat?. Whatever has happened to our flavouring the meats to tenderness naturally? I have so many questions, so many doubts.

They now serve meat flavorless of barbecue, camouflaged with red sauce they now call barbecue sauce. It looks like catchup. I agree it is a tasty flavour but to what barbecue means to tender and flavour. With desired spice seasoning, flame and wood smoke. Flavouring after the cook alone layers the taste and does not flavour meat internally. Its a short cut to over taste the meat presented. Smoking flavour into meat is achieved only with flame and hard wood, a true cooking method, not a topping over ice creame.

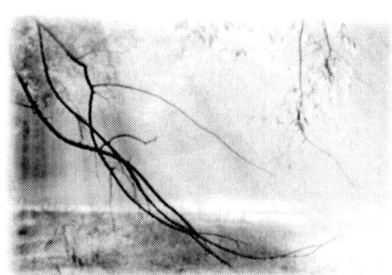

My displeasure prompts me to ask this question. Where did our tradition go? Has it left us all together? Is it now gone for the convenience of a rapid cook tyme?

Thankfully, one day in my travels, I found my answer. It is fully and completely NO!. You may still find the good in old style barbecue smokers in with traditional restaurers, public pub houses, and backyard fields. These are true people whom serve the wood marinade into the meat without a fancy reddish topping. I am now satisfied that I found many small country side towns, opposing the change to catchup based red sauce. Opposition is done not only to preserve a barbecue heritage personal to their family, but they knowingly are passing on their culture of the true barbecued meat......a tender flavoured with seasonings meat cooked over hours of tyme, fired in a low temperature wood smoker.

My wife Joyce and I spent some tyme traveling North of East Anglia to the town of Cromer, England when we found one such place that maintained a barbecue tradition. It was a special loving tyme for us to be together. In route to our destined site, we were distracted when as we caught sight of a smoke trail bellowing from the woodlands. The thickness of the smoke was as dense as a house fire. To be neighborly in our passing, we took emergency steps to assist, We quickly rerouted our horse buggy to the next available road leading towards the smoking sky. The road was bumpy and too harsh for our buggy and we considered a turn around but the thought of leaving someone in distress was too overcoming. So, delaying decision, we traveled another few hundred meters until turning onto a sharp bend onto a smoother road. This is where we spotted the smoke clearly creeping out of the hickory trees. Our hearts started racing as we got closer, only thinking of the unknown. Would we save a home, or a strangers jeopardized life in this fiery of danger? Not knowing what we were about to face, we focused on giving our hearts extra breaths of fresh air to relax it.

We traveled another three hundred meters until we fell upon a large opened grassland area, cut out from the streets edge to the hard wood timbers behind, looking as old as earths creation, the land held an old leaning wooden structure and a nearby aged restaurer family. I immediately saw the outer barn building with a homemade metal smoker made of scrap, blackened in color, and a topped brick exhaust stacked beyond the roofs top that steamed curled smoke way into the sky. My thought of danger was relieved to delight.

Two elderly men near the smoker, tended the pigs that sprawled across the spit and were wearing a thick double layer of old ragged clothes, seemingly unclean. These warn out garments covered them from head to toe also covering their feet as though it was their flame protector. I was confused by their garment selection since it was a very hot and very moist 90-degree day. In spite of this, I assumed quickly that they dressed so heavily for a reason, so whom am I to wonder. After all, I am witnessing a tradition.

Extruding aroma from the smoke was a pungent scent of hickory and oak wood mixed with pork flavour. It made my tongue pallet tingle with excitement. As we starting from being rescuers we now realize our situation, as being rescued, and so we laughed together loudly and immediately knew dinnertime was near. Not only was the air flavouring calling us into the building, the non painted building itself stated a place of comfort. I felt part of this small towns history. As we pulled onto the land, I noticed an abundance of empty buggies pulled near to the restaurers entrance. We knew we also had to enter its environment.

The building was packed with patrons whom stood along each available wall and congested every corner. To my surprise, we found a tiny mid-1800 wooden table placed in the pub area. Seating tightly, it almost seemed the patrons left it for courtesy of the guests. I immediately knew we found a special barbecue culture that would never change. My Lord, what a joy, what excitement, to find such a fine place!

We ordered the barbecued pulled pork from a member staff serving the table. Upon the serving, out came brown pork, pulled, not red.

Looking very pleased, Joyce asked; "Why did you not serve the new popular red sauce in your serving?"

The staff person replied friendly but snappily "Honey dear, we serve our tradition, not fake crusted flavour. If you wish to have the red sauce, it is in those bottle squeezers near the bar area. If you need em, go get em, use em, and return em. But, please first be aware that everyone is watching, placing bets on new comers to fall to the new sauce. Our taste is traditional barbecue. We call it "Brown and Tender.""

As I looked around to each table to dishes already served. I spoke calmly to Joyce that "no one has dared squeezed the red sauce onto their meat. I think those bottles are simply used as a gambling game to humor the locals."

So I suggested to Joyce that we let the gamblers lose their wager since they predict outsiders will select the red sauce and that our selection be the traditional, whilst honoring the servers request to eat it as it was intended. "After all," I said "she might have the winning bet."

Following the smoked sky was a decision made in heaven. We both found the location, its people, and its tradition most rewarding. It was the one of the most memorable times in our trip.

Sir Alfred John

Sir Alfred John

Tragedy

Michelena

Memoirs of Sir Alfred John......Michelena, A Wood Stove Tragedy
Michelena Castelli

Evelyn Chia born three daughters named Katherine, Julie, Joyce, and sons Douglas and Joseph, and an adopted family member nicknamed "Pie". At birth she was full of surprise constantly kicking and screaming in attempt to stretch her body longer. Reaching for understanding of life, her first words always started and ended with the question "why?"

 Pie's real name is Michelena Castelli. A beautiful little Italian angel with draping wavy dark black hair never cut since birth held deep brown pupils that mirrored what she was looking at would lay nestled between her natural curled eyelashes. A perfectly beautiful child enjoying life's simple pleasures but she never strayed from curiosity.

One late hot summer day, her family was preparing a Saturday evening dinner event for Michelena's next day birthday. All the neighbors were invited. The food selection was Pie's favorite, pizza. She found pizza a delight because she would create her own special mix of cheese, sauce, vegetables, and meats. Making pizza started with her imaging its delicious, delicate taste, prior to blending its preparation. The pizza would always hold delicate soft dough inside a hard surface crust with its toppings only Pie could combine. Its aroma would come from a brick covered wood fire stove heated with full smoke flavoured hard woods. Somehow she instinctively knew how to select the hard wood to scent the pizza with an aged flavor.

The oven was preheated and flamed with fire. Michelena was too young to tend it but on this special day of celebration she thought to increase the scent of the flavored wood. Her favorite wood scent was red maple. Unknowingly to us, she broke off a large sliver of wood from the nearby stack, opened the front door, and quickly threw the wood piece into the blaze.

Immediately when the wood hit the red hot flame it responded like the devil, violently rejecting the wood. In the flames torrent horror, it spewed back a few large chucks of red coal wooden chips onto Michelena clothes. One piece stuck to her beautiful newly made cotton pleaded birthday skirt. As it set aflame upon the skirt, it rapidly rose upward flaming her long hair and followed into the sky.

All of us assisted her in emergency; but we could not put out the flame within tyme. The wood piece she threw held an internal pocket of gas that exploded viciously as it hit the center of the flame.

In that tragic day, we lost our Pie, our Michelena. The sadness of our world caved in around us. When any of us lose offspring, friends, or those who touched us in some way, we can only grieve and come to God's conclusion of why we are put through this hardship. Some people are satisfied that a higher spiritual power made this choice, but for those with loss, do they understand or do they compromise the pain?

To me, loss comes only from old age, thus all other losses from accident, mishaps, or self decision are premature. Will your God grant your loss a spiritual life beyond the physical impurities of body, beyond our earth. Will mine? If I begin to believe there is reason, then I might understand. If I don't, then I will never be satisfied. I am in the crossroads of doubt. I might always be.

In the absence of my beliefs, I always know our love for our Pie will always be held in our hearts, our minds, and our blood. I pray daily that Michelena, our Pie, will get answers to her questions of "why" and with that knowledge. She will find the truth before me and this knowledge will make her a true angle.

Sir Alfred John

Michelena's Creations

Pizza Ingredients

Artichoke Turkey	Artichoke, Turkey, Garlic, Tomato
Bacon Cheeseburger	Ground Chuck, Onions, Tomato, Bacon, Mozzarella, Cheddar,
Lettuce	
BBQ Chicken	BBQ Sauce, Chicken Breast, Red Onions, Bacon, Mozzarella,
Cheddar	
Beef & Chile Pizza	Salsa, Beef, Mexican Cheese, Monterey, Green Chile Onion,
Cilantro	
Beef & Potato Pizza	Ground Beef, Potato Slices, BBQ Sauce, Cheddar
Black Bean Pizza	Black Bean, Salsa, Chicken, Tomato, Jalapeno, Mozzarella,
Cheddar	
Breakfast Pizza	EggsBacon or Sausage, Cheddar, Hash Browns, Parmesan,
Onion	
Canadian Bacon	Sauce, Canadian Bacon, Mozzarella, Mushroom, Red Bell,
Herbs	
Cheese Blend	Ricotta, Mozzarella, Asiago, Parmesan, Sauce or Olive Oil
Cordon Bleu Pizza	Parmesan Sauce, Fried Chicken, Ham, Swiss, Mozzarella
Eggplant Pizza	Sauce Eggplant, Mozzarella, Herbs
Formaggio	Gorgonzola, Asiago, Mozzarella, Pecorino, Basil
Goat Cheese	Walnut Oil, Goat Cheese, Walnuts, Tomato, Herbs
Leek & Cheese	Leek, Parsley, Tomato, Feta, Olive Oil, Butter, Herbs
Mediterranean	Olive Oil, Garlic, Tomato, Onion, Artichoke, Black Olive, Feta,
Herbs	
Mushroom & Olives	Sauce, Mozzarella, Mushrooms,, Olives
Pesto and Feta	Pesto Sauce, Olive Oil, Parsley, Garlic, Pine Nut, Parmesan,
Butter, Feta	
Pesto Pizza	Pesto Sauce, Tomato, Garlic, Mozzarella, Herbs
Pineapple Pizza	BBQ Sauce, Pineapple Slices, Ham, Bacon, Mozzarella
Potato Pizza	Sauce, Mashed Potato, Butter, Bacon, Onion, Mozzarella,
Cheddar	
Prosciutto White	Prosciutto, Olives, Garlic, Ricotta Cheese, Mozzarella, Olive Oil
RanchHand Pizza	BBQ Sauce, Turkey, Tomato,, Bacon, Mozzarella, Cheddar
Reuben Pizza	Thousand Island Sauce, Corned Beef, Sauerkraut, Swiss,
Mozzarella	

Sir Alfred John

Harmony

The World's Spice Mix

Memoirs of Sir Alfred John..........A World Combined

Long ago when I was a child, a year when winter was upon us, I heard that the new country Americas have countless plants, spices, and delicate flower flavours to delight our tastes. Will these become so better than our Great England India spices? Will our England and India merchant trade routes ruin with cargos diverted to the new land? What is this new soil offering?

Oh Lord, our England cannot afford such a trade diversion. It will be economically tragic if demand for our plants fall behind that of the new land. We are leaders of the spice trade with our port routes between England and the Indies. Our great England could lose its worldly dominance and make our economy problematic. Will these new spices prevail over my fellow citizens' desires and our lands be ignored? Or will this provide a new partner in trade and my economic fears fruitless of thought?

Oh Lord, please help in my success to preclude such disaster I must in my way, bring the best of these world flavours into one flavorful blend. I will introduce a perfect balance of plants to our merchant markets so to increase demand for our England spice and to avoid this economic struggle for our spice trade. I will make a global spice for all culinary persons of the world, uniting them together with one unique worldly flavor, so England maintains its domination . I will call it "A World Combined, The Universal Taste". This herb and spice flavour shall be so heavenly since the sun equally shares its power of light to all our earths' plants equally and each plant uniquely tasted to its enriched soil and climate.

We shall be proud to call ourselves men who share each other's culture. With success, many men in the world shall inter-mix thoughts and passions and possibly share equivalency in social advocacy, friendship and stature. This can become our countries best contribution to culinary, and our world spice trade.

I will go today and trade quickly with cargo Captains in port to purchase these new worldly plants. I will exhaustively blend the most perfect blend whether it takes me a day, months, years.

Oh Lord, it shall be done I tell you.... It shall be done.

Sir Alfred John

Sir Alfred John

Affliction

Plant Disease

Memoirs of Sir Alfred John.......... Thoughts of Plant Disease

Spices, ground sprouts, and fruits have become wonderful additions to flavouring our dishes. But I worry of mans progression in its distribution of such fine commodities along with the mixing of pest rats and other ship rodents. With such lucrative ways of work, I fear that greed may take our great spice and become bug ridden, unsafe for consumption, and ruin industries.

Will plants come into my Great England with disease or poisons similar to naturally tainted mushrooms? Will tomatoes be gardened too quickly and fall early from adult size? Will demand for fast plant growth call for something other than our precious soils an manures? With our population ever increasing so rapidly will our provisions fall short of demand?

I wait with cautiousness in witnessing this unfolding. Nevertheless in my lifetime, I may be lucky enough to not know these answers if such questions were true. I pray today to let my England's traditions pass on beyond my death and have faith in our society dedicating ourselves to the remembrance of our traditions, and our herbs.

For God's sake, for the health and safety of us all, may we avoid such displeasures.

Sir Alfred John

Sir Alfred John

Ideas

Potato Thoughts

Sir Alfred John Memoirs..........Quips of the Potato Patch

 Mothers viewpoint......What I know about potatoes is nothing. They boil, they bake, they fry, they dry, they mash, and they taste good with butter. All I want to do is eat them.

- Don't bug me about potatoes. Potatoes feed bugs and worms before humans. They ate well!

- Since I love potatoes so much, I'd like to establish this rule today; any animal whom eats a potato from my garden is worth putting in an evenings stew.

- Serve friends softly cooked potatoes often and they will return, serve unwanted guests less cooked potatoes.

- Potatoes grow in a dark soil and then grow the opposite in color.

- Potato skin has more than one purpose. I know its dirty so I cannot tell.

- How many feet of potatoes does it take to make it mashed? Only one foot!

- Each potatoes has a unique facial expression, each a personality. This one looks just like someone I know. He's a potato head!

- Place two potatoes together and it makes them a couple of spuds.

- Potatoes taste so unique when cut differently. Why?

- Will my potato patch feed my family next season or will drought come upon us?

- Are potatoes a fruit or vegetable? They are both.

- Are french fries from France?

- Is a Potato chip chipped?

- Shouldn't baked potatoes come from the bakery?

- Does double baked potatoes require two ovens?

- Why do potato chips not melt when placed in rain water?

- Is the word Potatoes actually referring to cooking a Pot of Toes?

- Farmers cross developed potatoes to reach new moistures and taste. They did good.

- Each potato is unique in size and expression. Each has a fingerprint.

- The only ultimate potato is the one your eating.

- Did you know? White potatoes replenished the energies of the Russian Red Army.

- Did you know? Potatoes advanced society. It was traded like money.

Sir Alfred John

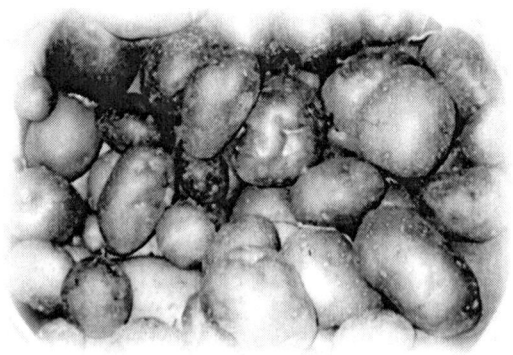

Sir Alfred John

Maturity

Turkey Thoughts

Memoirs of Sir Alfred John.........My Turkey Thoughts

I must be a turkey to have turkey thoughts. As I peruse my land in a hunt, I see the most plentiful wildly roaming turkeys that it would feast my dinner table daily. I look at them with a pointed bow and arrow as they are so easily to slay. They see me and slowly continue their search for seed within the nutrients of the grassland. The only escape for them is to fly heavily into the dense air so to reach distances beyond my reach. So clumsy in flight they lift with terrible grace spending enormous energy to lift to the air with their abundant weight. Their strength is to fly in a slow but seeming exhausting clip of pace that so to gain its escape from a hunters aim. Yet, if they get caught into the trap of hunters trust then they will perish as many do. But alas, this one passes the man who gets more pleasure out of seeing them in the wild as they are.

Sometimes in my youth, I think that I could have been such a turkey. With a not so sure inexperienced, not yet developed mind, I make up my out of tough reality with a desired vigor and playful energy that I can do anything. And it seems I can.

I find now that age dwindles the energy but replaces the youthful thoughts with strength of mind. A reversal of mind and body to survive the daily vigor of life. I have to think the the wild turkey has to do the same, although their mind is not so large but in a way similar to ours in aging. If this is true which the older wild turkeys seem to say, then with my elder years upon me, I profess to have turkey thoughts.

Sir Alfred John

Sir Alfred John

Evolution

First the Chicken; Second the Evolution

Memoirs of Sir Alfred John..........The Protective Shell

As I sit resting in my hen house, I ponder........was the chicken born, or was the egg laid, which proceeded the other? It's a scientific mystery to our evolution. It's an inquiry to natures battle to create balance.

I desire in my memoir today to express my beliefs and record my thoughts. Older and wiser now allows me to determine these facts. My fellow countrymen may disagree or be anger at my conclusion but no doubt that my opinion shall stand clear and concise when the discovery is found. If ever found.

We should all however respect opinions of others for the unknown.

As human species we live in physical body. Prior to reproduction, we can only exist in physical matter within the womb. Similarly new borne chickens, hens, or roosters, can only be borne from physical body and dispersed in a non-shelled event. I believe that the hardshell is one of the greatness evolutions on our earth. Since the originating species born similar to us, they thought it wise to protect their new borne with hard shell. So it changed its process of birth. In this evolution, massive bird destruction from predators like fox, rats, and infection directed poultry to hardshell its new born for protection of extinction.

I am convinced when I see the hen bird reaching toward the hardshell to smell and seemingly chip onto the shell to communicate its newborn. As they look in puzzlement of such hardshell it seems they were expecting something different.

Only a motherly spirit could penetrate sound to this imprisonment to tell the newborn there is life waiting, and to anticipate its breath for first air.

In comparison of its evolution, we humankind developed greatness only recently by reaching proper of philosophical thought and invention. We not know totally of our genealogy or detail our relationship to our eldest ancestors; but know only our recent beginnings and our most recent forefathers, mothers, and children. One thing is clear, our ancestors advanced their level of sophistication and social class only after sustaining the need of basic skills in survival. Writing of history they taught through voice and verbalization as our great paper and pen was not available to them. Teaching therefore, is a form of evolution. We change our environment and our bodies through knowledge and skill of surgeons. We live longer through cleansing and medications. We think higher thought and a new idea is learned. This is our evolution.

My belief is that our foremothers repeating births provided our evolutional change over time, similar to the hen that had to build a hard shell to homestead its newborn from predators.

Traditional hen protects its young with a hardshell and that gives it protection. But when the adult hen life's is threatened by prey, the adult hen easily gives up its shelled egg expecting the shell to protect it. Which sometime it does.

In comparison, over tyme our age, our mothers release us freely to the world of predators that they call adulthood. And, in our adult life, we must defend ourselves in our "shells of armor."

Sir Alfred John

Sir Alfred John

Equality

Tranquility

Memoirs of Sir Alfred John.........One Day of Equality

For a few days now, my farm duties have become less important than the days prior. It is so unordinary for me, a weighted strong man, succumbing to a day of rest instead of realizing my farm duties. My wondering mind today cannot comprehend the importance of my chores. Many days prior to today, I sighted sections of my land not presentable to its usual attractiveness and in need of care. Nevertheless, today, the untamed land has grown a colorful wild beauty upon its ridges and the sun reflects against the dancing grass seemingly brings the pasture new pleasures

I am confused this day by the comfort of this vision. Self-assessment of what I see and feel suggests that serenity is upon me, but how can this be true? Exciting is the newborn vision of beauty of what I've seen previously. Remembering bits and pieces of my great land are now connected with enhanced colors and streaming patterns The land seems connected from my feet to the sky. But, why is this? What is happening to me? Why are my eyes distinguishing my thoughts differently today than it did so just yesterday? I wonder this with enthusiasm and the hopeful pleasure of feeling this tomorrow.

Feeling so tranquil, with ache-free muscles, lazy, and confident thoughts, I decided today to rest atop the North Fence where there is a unlimited views of sun, water, grass, and earth. Today, I feel that there is so much balance between the earth and me that this sitting position is all I can muster. What is happening to me? I have never felt this subtleness in the past. Why now, why today?

I've heard traveling patrons and others speak of such a hearted occasion. They say only a few persons of population attached to this world will be a fortunate man and become equivalent to his land, so as to form a spiritual bond and ghostly partnership to our earth. They say that such men will find self reliance in a relationship to the loving natural beauty of earth's soil. They say it is rare and most pleasing if you are chosen to feel, and be felt. But today, is it my day? Can it be? It must be. I feel a harmonized heartbeat through the grass fields as though the earthly winds play its music within.

Looking across the land, I see new spectrum of imaginative colorings entering my eyes. Have I turned my eyes blind from this in the past? I now see light shades freely bouncing off the calm waters of Lena's pond, creating newborn rainbows heading east to the days originating sun. I see the deepest of colors in trees, not only its outer edges, but even dark shaded colors of the inner shell. I do not recall seeing arms stemming through the trees that sprawl from its center to its outer shell and protective cover. I see clearly a sharp separation of clear blue-skies held up only with a foundation of green land, with floating deep white puffy clouds of cotton moving slowly across.

For this moment, if it brief, my wish is my healed eyes shall never wear glass spectacles as I age. Only others will have to magnify their vision since I can now see so perfectly.

Resting upon my bench embraced by this calmness and tranquility of Gods land, and losing many productive farm hours today, I welcome this comfort to be upon me forever. I'm hopeful my new founded comfort with tranquility will be with me another day, maybe, just maybe, as early as tomorrow.

Sir Alfred John

Sir Alfred John

Characterization

Characters

The name Sir Alfred John is a fictitious name made up by combining Sir Alfred Munnings, PPRA and Captain Sir John Seaman. Sir Alfred Munnings is a renowned painter in England and his painting of his friend, Captain Sir John Seaman became the inspiration for the books title. In searching my genealogy I traced my descendants path to olde England. The trail is absolute to the where my fathers father came from as the generations are named similarly. The connection to me has not yet been determined but the connection between them is undoubtedly true as that story is told through a Sir Alfred Munnings portrait of Captain Sir John Seaman. I hold the painting.

These memoirs and stories represent an autobiography of my life, my families and friends lives, and its adventures. The book portrays the location where Sir Alfred Munnings lived in his tyme in his olde England.

Sir Alfred John spice can be found on the internet at www.SirAlfredJohn.com.

Below is the list of characters used in this book and their relationship to the book, person, or family.

Ana Rosé	My mother
Another man's land	Do not trespass, otherwise suffer the consequences
Antonio and Rosé Marie	Two persons who love each other, together or not
Baconly	A porky friend of the family
Balanced Rock	A special place for Joyce and I
Blue Whale	Almost extinct, well respected worldwide
Bugs, sea bugs	Shrimp, and more shrimp
Captain John	Captain John Seaman, a Ship Captain,
best	friend of SAJ
Cattle Boss	Norman, always enjoying the fields sport

Citizens	Townspeople
Creation	Learn sausage making
Crew	People finding destiny while floating on seawater
Denise	Sir Willard's daughter, Cousin Bill's daughter
Edward Thomas Boardman	Library Owner
Egg	Fowls gift to breakfast
Homestead women	Women who did not participate in the hunt
I	Me or Sir Alfred John
Importers and sea merchants	Pirates or honest men trying to make a sea trade living
Joyce	My wife, Sir Alfred John's wife
Lady Norma	Roberts wife
Lena's pond	Sister Lena's favorite pond. She was laid to rest near it
Loving creatures are Gods	All life on earth
Madam Kat	My wife's sister, my sister in law
Man hunter	Person responsible to find food, & some women
Michael; Neighbor of SAJ	The boy inside the Author
Michael	The Author
Michol	A German Shepherd, in my life for six years
Michelena Castelli	Sister of my Mother who died in wood stove fire
Molly's fine drink	A favorite alcoholic juice
Mother	Mom, woman who gave me life
My father	Birth father, ruler of discipline, and wage earner
My wife and I	Respect by placing wife in language first
Norman	Cattle drive boss, favorite uncle
Old tyme rancher	A herdsman or farmer experienced or later in years
Patricia Evelyn (Chia)	Mother of my wife Joyce
People and buggies	A new found love of travel
Persons of standing	Those who got there prior, or in stature
Piedo white	My young warm-hearted sister Denise's rabbit
Practitioner be	Practicing what they preach, but may not correct
Predators	Man, fox, other prey known to kill settled animals

Red Army of Workers and Peasants	Established in Russia to fight their cause
RanchHands Field spectacular	Where Southside Bench overlooks views
Romaine living	Sir Alfred Johns child, Grandpas only daughter
Romaine	Lettuce
Scrimshaw vessel	Old time vessel designed for cargo
Sea shrimp	Captain John's Fish Bugs
Sir Alfred John spices	Brand name of spices, marinades and rubs
Sir Higgins	Sir Alfred Johns ranch Manager, married to Romaine
Sir Norman	Ranch Hand, Authors favorite Uncle
Sir Raymond	Dad
Sir Robert Fireman	Neighbor of Romaine, Uncle Bob the Fireman
Sir Robert and Lady Norma Jean	Married, fun loving and attracted to ladders.
Sir Willard cream	Cousin of Dad, memories of the ice parlor
Southside Bench resting	In RanchHands Field, a ranch hands place
The Chicken	Fowl
The Harbormaster	Someone who looks for boats in trouble
The New Calf	A fresh bourn Betsy Junior
The Ranch Manager	Person in charge to relieve owner of duties
Trotter	Sir Alfred John's favorite horse
Two cows wandered away	Cow Betsy and Sir Cow Stanley
Unseen barbarous creature	A little fish playing brain games
Unwanted attack animals	An aggressive animal or human without conscience
We	Everyone involved
Wife of Sir Alfred John	Joyce C. Maffeo
Worm strings	Fish bait that look like drowning brown

Olde Maps of England

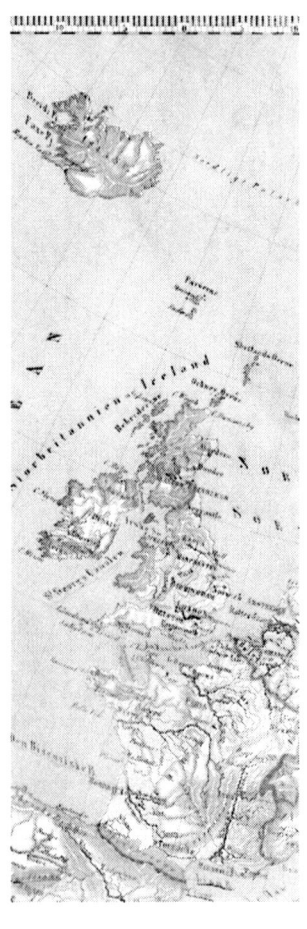

Europe in 1867
Map of Europe
scanned from a
hand-coloured map

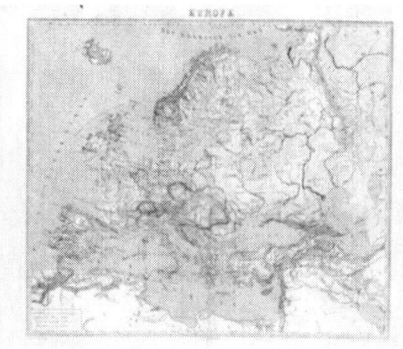

CPSIA information can be obtained at www.ICGtesting.com
Printed in the USA
LVOW121633041212

309908LV00022BA/1362/P